Growing Readers

Pearl's First Prize Plant

Story and illustrations by A. Delaney

📚 HarperCollins*Publishers*

Library of Congress Cataloging-in-Publication Data
Delaney, A.
    Pearl's first prize plant / story and illustrations by A. Delaney.
        p.   cm.
    Summary: A young girl plants a seed, watches it grow, and enters
it in the county fair plant show.
    ISBN 0-06-027356-9. — ISBN 0-06-027357-7 (lib. bdg.)
    [1. Gardening—Fiction.]   I. Title.
PZ7.D37318Pe   1997   96-2223
[E]—dc20   CIP
                                                          AC

Typography by Anna Raff
1   2   3   4   5   6   7   8   9   10
❖
First Edition

To David

One day in spring,

Pearl planted a seed.

Day by day, Pearl watched the seed grow

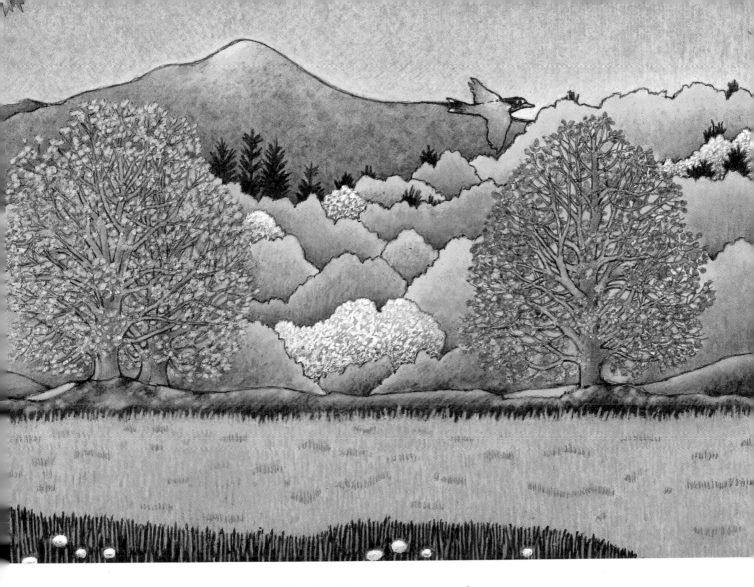

into a little green plant.

Pearl took very good care of her plant.

It grew and grew.

One day, the little green plant

grew a little white flower.

"Wow!" said Pearl.

"You are the best plant I ever saw!"

Pearl took the little green plant

to the county fair.

She knew it would win First Prize at the Flower Show.

"Oh, no!" said Pearl.

Pearl looked at the red flowers.

She looked at the orange flowers.

She looked at the yellow flowers

and at the blue flowers.

She looked at the purple flowers.

Then Pearl looked at her own little green plant,
with its little white flower.

"Hmph!" she said. And that was that!

Pearl took her plant home

and planted it by an old tree.

"You're *my* First Prize Plant!" she said.

The rain rained. The sun shone.

And Pearl and her First Prize Plant were as happy as could be!